absolute mayhem

Written and Illustrated By
Kelly Suellentrop

Striped Socks Publishing

ISBN 978-0692311011

Printed in the United States of America.

Published by
Striped Socks Publishing
P.O. Box 911
Manchester, MO 63011

Visit Kelly Suellentrop at: www.kellysuellentrop.com

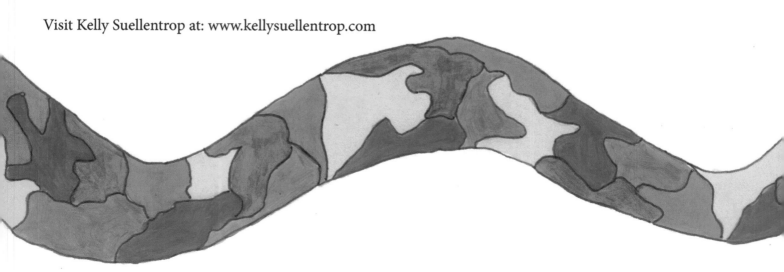

To Kurt
for giving the Mayhem a name

To Grace
& Michael
for giving the Mayhem life

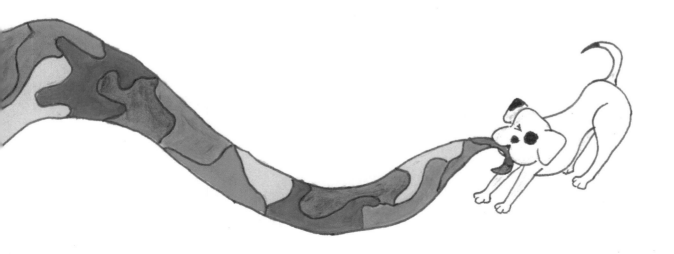

The grown-up world is the ultimate bore,
Full of errands,
and tasks,
and lists to do.
There is always work that needs to be done.
Lulu and Milo must do their part, too.

It's hard to do everything they are told,
Behave like good kids and always obey.
But Lulu and Milo know that quite soon
Their days will be filled with nothing but play.

During the week, they live by the rules
And work on dull chores expected of them.
But when Friday evening rolls around,
Everything turns to Absolute Mayhem!

Absolute Mayhem means fun rules the day,
The night is filled with magic and wonder.
And things that are normal during the week
Turn to crazy creations of splendor.

Throughout the week, Lulu works hard
On grammar, math facts, and spelling review.
Yet Absolute Mayhem transforms her thoughts,
And her mind creates worlds she escapes to...

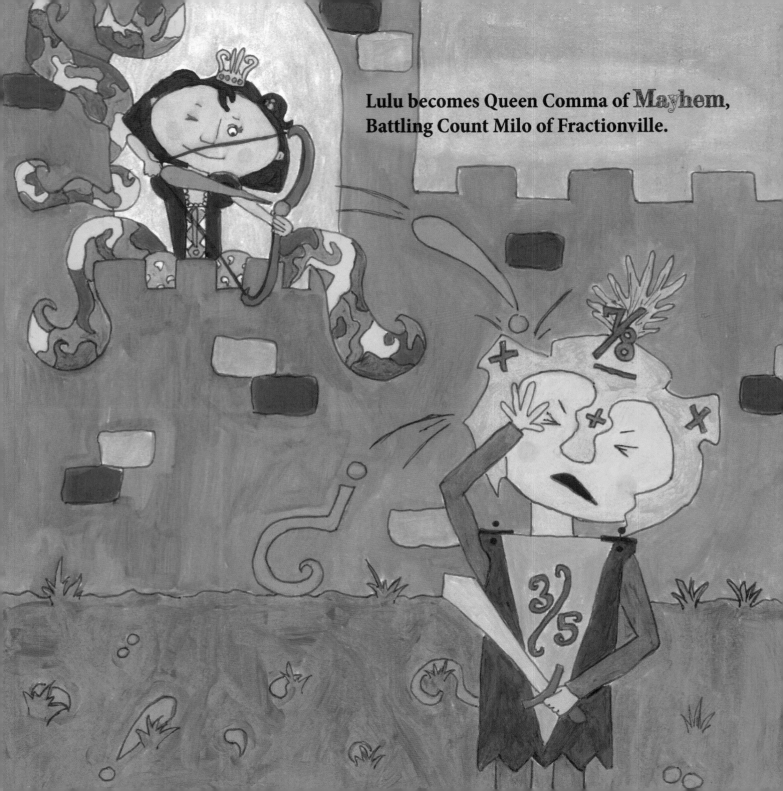

Lulu becomes Queen Comma of Mayhem,
Battling Count Milo of Fractionville.

She rules the Palace of Punctuation
And orders him to endless writing drills.

On most days Milo struggles through dinner,
Choking down veggies in various ways.
Absolute Mayhem's menu is different,
Sending him into a sugary daze...

Candy can be munched on at every meal,
Monday's plain milk becomes Mayhem's milkshake.

Tuesday's bland turnips are instead swapped for
Cream of sprinkles soup with a side of cupcakes.

On Wednesdays Lulu must take out the trash,
And Milo must clean up the dog's doo-doo.
But chores don't exist in Absolute Mayhem,
So everyone can do as they want to...

Lulu spends weekends as an explorer,
Finding jewels in such deep and dark places.

Milo plays zookeeper tending to beasts,
Tidying up their habitat spaces.

On nights like Thursday, it's to bed by eight.
So Lulu and Milo hit the sack hard.
For Absolute Mayhem they camp beneath stars,
As a jungle overcomes the backyard...

They barricade themselves inside their tent,
Listening to untamed sounds of the night.
They laugh at monkeys scavenging outside,
While stuffed in sleeping bags, snuggled tight.

During the week, their dreams are fantastic.
Minds run wild all night until they ache.

Dreams aren't needed in **Absolute Mayhem.**
They live imagination while awake.

Absolute Mayhem makes weekdays seem dull,
Since playing themselves silly is so grand.
But soon the **Mayhem** has taken control,
And everything gets a bit out of hand.

Lulu is too pooped to keep order as Queen.
Milo's tummy hurts from the sweet buffet.
The backyard monkeys are flinging cupcakes...

It's a good thing tomorrow is Monday.

About the Author

Kelly Suellentrop is an author and an illustrator, which are the two exact things she always wanted to be when she grew up. But she also would not mind being a professional roller coaster rider, a tour guide at Graceland, or the drummer in a band…if only she knew how to play the drums. She lives in St. Louis, Missouri with her husband and their two children, one girl and one boy…who may or may not bear a resemblance to Lulu and Milo.

Visit Kelly, Lulu, and Milo at www.kellysuellentrop.com

photo © Erich Suellentrop

Like this book? Lulu and Milo want to hear what you think!
Please leave a customer review on Amazon.com

Made in the USA
Lexington, KY
12 December 2015